ASTERIX AN CHIEFTAIN'S SHIELD

TEXT BY GOSCINNY

DRAWINGS BY UDERZO

TRANSLATED BY ANTHEA BELL AND DEREK HOCKRIDGE

KNIGHT BOOKS
Hodder & Stoughton

Copyright © Dargaud Editeur 1968
English Language text copyright © Hodder & Stoughton
Ltd 1977

First published in Great Britain 1977 (cased)
by Hodder & Stoughton Children's Books

This edition first published 1981 by Knight Books,
Hodder Dargaud

Third impression 1984

Printed and bound in Belgium for Hodder Dargaud Ltd.,
Mill Road, Dunton Green, Sevenoaks, Kent (Editorial Office:
47 Bedford Square, London, WC1B 3DP) by
Henri Proost & Cie, Turnhout

ISBN 0 340 26469 1

The year is 50 BC. Gaul is entirely occupied by the Romans.
Well, not entirely... One small village of indomitable Gauls still
holds out against the invaders. And life is not easy for the
Roman legionaries who garrison the fortified camps of
Totorum, Aquarium, Laudanum and Compendium...

a few of the Gauls

Asterix, the hero of these adventures. A shrewd, cunning little warrior; all perilous missions are immediately entrusted to him. Asterix gets his superhuman strength from the magic potion brewed by the druid Getafix...

Obelix, Asterix's inseparable friend. A menhir delivery-man by trade; addicted to wild boar. Obelix is always ready to drop everything and go off on a new adventure with Asterix – so long as there's wild boar to eat, and plenty of fighting.

Getafix, the venerable village druid. Gathers mistletoe and brews magic potions. His speciality is the potion which gives the drinker superhuman strength. But Getafix also has other recipes up his sleeve...

Cacofonix, the bard. Opinion is divided as to his musical gifts. Cacofonix thinks he's a genius. Everyone else thinks he's unspeakable. But so long as he doesn't speak, let alone sing, everybody likes him...

Finally, Vitalstatistix, the chief of the tribe. Majestic, brave and hot-tempered, the old warrior is respected by his men and feared by his enemies. Vitalstatistix himself has only one fear; he is afraid the sky may fall on his head tomorrow. But as he always says, 'Tomorrow never comes.'

...RCINGETORIX, DEFEATED AT [T]E SIEGE OF ALESIA, THROWS HIS [AR]MS AT CAESAR'S FEET... AND [OFFI]CIALLY, ALL GAUL IS CONQUERED...

OUCH!

CLANG!

AFTER THIS MELANCHOLY CEREMONY, CAESAR SETS OFF IN SEARCH OF FRESH CONQUESTS ...

...AND THE ARMS OF THE [AR]VERNIAN CHIEFTAIN LIE [WH]ERE THEY HAVE FALLEN. [N]ONE DARES TOUCH THEM...

... UNTIL SUNSET, WHEN A ROMAN ARCHER SUCCUMBS TO TEMPTATION AND MAKES OFF WITH A MAGNIFICENT SHIELD...

HEY, HOW ABOUT A GAME OF RUBER ET NIGER?

!

...WHICH HE LOSES AT ONCE IN [A] GAME OF CHANCE.

DIEM PERDIDI!

YOU CAN QUOTE ME ON THAT TOO!

THE WINNER, A LEGIONARY OUT WITHOUT A PASS, FINDS THE PRESENT TENSE WHEN TRYING TO SNEAK INTO CAMP, HE IS PICKED UP BY A CENTURION WITH AN ACTIVE VOICE...

HEY, YOU THERE! QUO VADIS, LADDIE?

... AND IN AN IMPERATIVE MOOD, WHO CONFISCATES THE SHIELD IN RETURN FOR HIS SILENCE...

O TEMPORA! O MORES!

... [THE] CENTURION, HAVING SPENT ALL HIS PAY, [SW]OPS THE PRECIOUS SHIELD FOR AN [AM]PHORA OF WINE AT A WINE AND [CH]ARCOAL MERCHANTS ...

... AND THE SHOPKEEPER SUBSEQUENTLY AGREES TO HAND IT OVER TO A GAULISH WARRIOR WHO HAS ESCAPED FROM ALESIA ...

... AND IS TRYING TO DROWN HIS SORROWS IN DRINK ...

WELL, IF IT GIVES YOU ANY SATISFACTION...

HIC!

SO ALL GAUL IS OCCUPIED. ALL? NO! ONE LITTLE GAULISH VILLAGE IS STILL HOLDING OUT AGAINST THE INVADERS. A LITTLE VILLAGE WE KNOW VERY WELL, WHERE MORALE IS HIGH, AND ANY EXCUSE WILL DO TO HOLD A BANQUET WITH LOTS TO EAT AND DRINK. AS IT HAPPENS, THE LAST SUCH BANQUET HAS HAD SOME UNFORTUNATE CONSEQUENCES...

OOOOW! OOOOOOH! OH! OH! OH!

IS SOMEONE SLAUGHTERING A WILD BOAR?

NO, IT'S OUR BARD SINGING A LULLABY!

MAKE WAY FOR THE DRUID! CHIEF VITALSTATISTIX IS ILL!

IT'S THE SAME OLD STORY: THE DAY AFTER HE'S BEEN EATING AND DRINKING AND MAKING MERRY WITH THOSE BARBARIANS HE FEELS AS IF THE SKY HAD FALLEN ON HIS HEAD!

IT ISN'T MY HEAD THAT HURTS!

DOES IT HURT THERE, THEN?

AH, YES, HE'S GOT LIVER TROUBLE!

I NEVER KNEW ANYONE COULD GET LIVER TROUBLE...

OUUCH!

I WISH I WAS DEAD!

YOUR WIFE IMPEDIMENTA IS RIGHT, O CHIEF, I'M AFRAID YOU ATE AND DRANK RATHER TOO MUCH AT OUR LAST BANQUET.

I NEVER KNEW ANYONE COULD EAT TOO MUCH.

7

I WOULDN'T MIND A HOLIDAY IN THOSE PARTS...

RIGHT, I'M GOING TO SEND YOU TO SEE THE DRUID DIAGNOSTIX, WHO RUNS THE FAMOUS HYDRO AT AQUAE CALIDAE.

AND WE'LL GO WITH YOU, O VITAL STATISTIX! A CHIEF OUGHT TO HAVE AN ESCORT!

YES, AND DOGMATIX CAN COME TOO! A SLIMMING CURE MIGHT DO HIM GOOD. HE'S GETTING FAT.

THE CHIEF'S LIVER IS SOON SOOTHED BY SOME INFUSIONS BREWED BY GETAFIX. PREPARATIONS FOR THE JOURNEY ARE GOING AHEAD; ASTERIX HAS BEEN GIVEN HIS GOURD OF MAGIC POTION AND OBELIX IS SULKING SLIGHTLY...

I KNOW, I KNOW, I DON'T GET ANY BECAUSE GNGNGN GNGNGN...

I'M A BIT SORRY TO LEAVE THE VILLAGE, BUT WE CAN HAVE A GREAT BANQUET TO CELEBRATE OUR DEPARTURE AND...

BANQUET? I'M SICK AND TIRED OF SACRIFICING MYSELF FOR A GREAT FAT BARBARIAN WITHOUT THE GUMPTION OF A WILD BOAR PIGLET...

...WHO DOESN'T SHOW ME THE LEAST CONSIDERATION AFTER I'VE GIVEN HIM THE BEST YEARS OF MY L...

COME ON, BOYS, LET'S GO.

THEY'RE... THEY'RE GOING! WITHOUT TELLING ANYONE!

CACOFONIX! CACOFONIX!

THE CHIEF'S OFF, WITH ASTERIX AND OBELIX!

HMPH? WHAT?

QUICK! I WILL NOW GIVE THEM A SONG OF...

OH NO, YOU WON'T! OH NO, YOU WON'T!

GOT THE ITINERARY?

YES, ASTERIX, AND THIS SLAB LISTS ALL THE BEST INNS ALONG OUR WAY.

BUT AREN'T YOU SUPPOSED TO BE ON A DIET?

WELL, IF I'M GOING TO HAVE A COURSE OF TREATMENT I MIGHT AS WELL MAKE IT WORTH WHILE. ANYWAY, THAT'S ALL ROT; I FEEL FINE. I WAS SUFFERING FROM A SPOT OF MENTAL FATIGUE, THAT'S ALL.

THERE! I ALWAYS KNEW EATING COULDN'T MAKE ANYONE ILL!

...AND THE JOURNEY BECOMES A GASTRONOMIC TOUR, WITH BANQUET FOLLOWING BANQUET...

GOOD FOOD NEVER HURT ANYONE, MY LADS...

SCRUNCH!

SCRUNCH!

...PUNCTUATED BY THE WISE AND MORALLY ELEVATING MAXIMS OF VITALSTATISTIX...

...SO LONG AS YOU DON'T GO TOO HEAVY ON THE SAUCES.

...MANY OF THEM STILL CURRENT TODAY AMONG PEOPLE ON A STRICT DIET.

USE A LITTLE WINE FOR THY STOMACH'S SAKE!

GLOUGLOU GLOU

...AND SO, IN DUE COURSE ...

LET GOOD DIGESTION WAIT ON APPETITE ...

SCRUNCH! SCRUNCH!

...OUR FRIENDS ARRIVE AT THE GATES OF AQUAE CALIDAE, THE END OF THEIR JOURNEY.

...AND CHEESE IS AN AID TO DIGESTION.

I'LL JUST HAVE A LITTLE NAP UNDER THAT TREE, BOYS. MY HEAD FEELS A BIT HEAVY ...

?!

NNNNN

BL BL BL BL BL

OOOUÜUUCH!

AND SO OUR FRIENDS ENTER THE *TOWN* OF AQUAE CALIDAE, FAMOUS AMONG BOTH GAULS AND ROMANS FOR *ITS* HOT SPRINGS AND MINERAL WATERS.

OOOOOOH! I WISH I WAS DEAD!

DIAGNOSTIX THE DRUID? THAT WAY. TELL HIM ABOUT YOUR CONDITION: WHATEVER SPRINGS TO MIND. I'VE GOT TO MIND THE SPRINGS.

SOON AFTERWARDS....

OUR DRUID GETAFIX HAS SENT US. IT'S ABOUT YOUR COURSE OF TREATMENT.

AH, EXCELLENT! AND WHICH OF YOU IS THE INVALID?

FOR THE ANSWER, PRESS HERE....

NO!

EXCELLENT, VERY GOOD! I WILL EXAMINE THE PATIENT.

NOOOOO! DON'T TOUCH ME! DON'T LOOK AT ME! IT HURTS!

HMM... A VERY SEVERE CASE. DIET N° 1

AND WHAT ABOUT YOU?

I'M FINE.

YOUR FAT FRIEND HERE OBVIOUSLY OVEREATS; I DOUBT IF HIS LIVER IS IN A HEALTHY *STATE*.

HE ISN'T FAT AND HIS LIVER IS IN A VERY GOOD STATE!

HE IS FAT, AND WE'LL SOON SEE ABOUT THE STATE OF HIS LIVER!

WHO ARE YOU TALKING ABOUT?

OOOOOOH!

TCHONC!

DRUID, QUICK! OUR CHIEF HAS FAINTED!

???

PAT! PAT! PAT!

10

VITALSTATISTIX STARTS HIS TREATMENT. HE DRINKS THE WATER OF THE SPRINGS AT REGULAR INTERVALS...

... USES THE SOPHISTICATED MODERN SHOWER SYSTEM...

SPLATCH!

... AND STICKS TO A STRICT DIET BASED ON BOILED VEGETABLES.

AND THIS IS WHERE THE TROUBLE BEGINS, SINCE ASTERIX AND OBELIX, AS THE CHIEF'S ESCORT, HAVE PERMISSION TO SHARE HIS TABLE AT MEAL TIMES...

HEY THERE! ANOTHER BOAR!

SNAP!

AND MORE BEER!

SOME OF THE OTHER PATIENTS BEGIN TO CRACK UP...

BOO...BOOHOOOHOOO!

AND SERIOUS INCIDENTS ARE ONLY JUST AVERTED.

IF YOU GO TAKING ADVANTAGE OF HIM TO STEAL HIS BONE BECAUSE HE'S SO SMALL I SHALL POKE YOU IN THE LIVER WITH MY FINGER!

GRRRR!

THE TREATMENT INCLUDES BATHING IN WATER FROM THE HOT SPRINGS.

IS IT NICE?

HMPFF!

HEY, ASTERIX, I'D LIKE TO TAKE A DIVE!

OBELIX, NOOOO!

SPLOSH!

WE'VE COME TO SAY GOODBYE, CHIEF VITALSTATISTIX.

WE'RE GOING TO HAVE A NICE HOLIDAY!

WELL, WE'RE OFF, O CHIEF. LOOK AFTER YOURSELF! WE'LL SEE YOU IN GERGOVIA WHEN YOUR TREATMENT'S OVER.

AND DON'T YOU WORRY ABOUT US. WE'RE GOING TO EXPLORE THE COUNTRYSIDE. I HEAR THE ARVERNIANS HAVE SOME GOOD LOCAL SPECIALITIES... WILD BOAR IN WINE...

AND VEGETABLE SOUP!

AND SAUSAGES!

GET OUT!

...AND THERE'S ARVERNIAN BLUE CHEESE...

COME ON, OBELIX. I THINK WE'D BETTER GET GOING!

AT THAT VERY MOMENT, IN THE KITCHENS OF THE HYDRO...

FUNNY.... THE PATIENTS SEEM RATHER QUIET!

?!

BONG!

I DON'T KNOW WHAT'S COME OVER THEM! WHEN I TOOK THE BOILED VEGETABLES IN THEY STARTED ACTING LIKE MADMEN! TWO OR THREE OF THEM EVEN BIT ME!

MEANWHILE OUR FRIENDS ARE STROLLING THROUGH THE BEAUTIFUL ARVERNIAN COUNTRYSIDE...

MARVELLOUS AIR UP HERE, OBELIX!

YES, BUT THERE'S ONE THING MISSING ... WE HAVEN'T SEEN MANY ROMAN LEGIONARIES LATELY.

MOVE ASIDE THERE, GAULS! MAKE WAY FOR TRIBUNE NOXIUS VAPUS, SPECIAL ENVOY OF JULIUS CAESAR!

?

DIDN'T YOU HEAR ME, GAULS? MAKE WAY FOR TRIBUNE NOXIUS VAPUS, SPECIAL ENVOY OF JULIUS CAESAR!

OH, GOODY! I LIKE THIS PLACE, ASTERIX. THEY'VE GOT EVERYTHING LAID ON! DO WE MAKE WAY?

WAIT A MOMENT... I'LL JUST TAKE A SPOT OF MAGIC POTION...

GLUG! GLUG! GLUG!

NO, WE DO NOT MAKE WAY! THEY DIDN'T ASK NICELY, SO WHY SHOULD WE?

YOU MOVE ASIDE, ROMANS! MAKE WAY FOR OBELIX, ASTERIX...

WOOF!

?!

... AND DOGMATIX, SPECIAL ENVOYS OF VITALSTATISTIX!

SLAUGHTER THOSE THREE IDIOTS BY JUPITER, AND LET GET ON WITH OUR JOURNEY!

LEGIONA...

BONG!

WHAT ARE THE OTHERS WAITING FOR?

YOU STARTED TOO SOON! THAT WAS THE HEAD OF THE SQUAD. PEOPLE WHO LOSE THEIR HEADS DON'T KNOW WHAT TO DO!

OH, WELL, ONCE MORE UNTO THE BREACH... COME ON, MEN.

CHARGE!

GOOD IDEA... CHARGE!

CHARGE! CHARGE!

YOU KNOW, OBELIX, IF ONLY EVERYONE ACTED LIKE THIS IT WOULD INCREASE INTERNATIONAL UNDERSTANDING NO END.

VADE RETRO!
AUDACES FORTUNA
JUVAT!

RIGHT.

17

19

Panel 1: I WONDER IF BOAR WOULD TASTE NICE IN THAT SOUP?

Panel 2: MOVE ASIDE, GAULS! MAKE WAY FOR TRIBUNE NOXIUS VAPUS, SPECIAL ENVOY OF JULIUS CAESAR!

Panel 3: WASN'T THAT THE NAME OF THAT ROMAN NUT-CASE, ASTERIX?

IF SO, WE'VE HAD A CRACK AT HIM BEFORE.

Panel 4: WANT TO GO AND SEE?

WHY NOT? AFTER ALL, WE'RE ON HOLIDAY.

Panel 5: SOON AFTERWARDS...

YES, THAT WAS HIM ALL RIGHT.

IT'S ALWAYS NICE TO MEET AN OLD FRIEND ON HOLIDAY.

16

Panel 6: MOST ROMANS COME TO THESE PARTS TO TAKE THE WATERS... I SEEM TO BE THE ONLY ONE WHO COMES HERE TO TAKE PUNISHMENT!

Panel 7: NICE LITTLE PLACE YOU'VE GOT HERE... AND EVERYTHING LAID ON IN THESE FORESTS: BOARS, NUTS, THE LOT.

WINESANSPIRIX

Panel 8: AND SPEAKING OF NUTS, WE RAN INTO THAT ROMAN FRIEND OF YOURS, BY LUG AND TOUTATIS.

VAPUS? VAPUS IS BACK? I DON'T LIKE THE SOUND OF THAT... WE MUST KEEP OUR LUGHOLES TO THE GROUND!

16

VAPUS IS NOTORIOUS IN THESE PARTS. CAESAR SENDS HIM TO KEEP US DOWN. IF HE'S BACK, WE'RE IN FOR A BAD TIME!

OH, DON'T LET'S BOTHER ABOUT A LITTLE THING LIKE THAT!

IT'S A REAL PLEASURE TO COOK FOR A MAN WHO ENJOYS HIS FOOD!

OH, I SAY!

MEANWHILE, TRIBUNE NOXIUS VAPUS ARRIVES AT THE PREFECT'S PALACE...

?

AVE, NOXIUS VAPUS! I DIDN'T EXPECT YOU BACK SO SOON...ER...DID YOU HAVE A GOOD JOURNEY?

SUMMON ALL THE COMMANDING OFFICERS OF THE LOCAL GARRISONS AT ONCE. ALL LEAVE IS CANCELLED!

HEAR THAT? JOIN UP, THEY SAID. IT'S A MAN'S LIFE, THEY SAID...

SOON AFTERWARDS...

WELL, THOSE ARE YOUR ORDERS: FIND THE CHIEFTAIN'S SHIELD SO THAT CAESAR CAN HOLD HIS TRIUMPH IN GERGOVIA!

A LOT OF ALESIANS CAME TO LIVE IN GERGOVIA AFTER THEIR DEFEAT. THAT GIVES US A GOOD OPENING. SEARCH EVERY HOUSE! AND GET MOVING, BY JUPITER!

WHY DON'T WE SEND CAESAR ANOTHER SHIELD? WE COULD TELL HIM IT WAS THE CHIEFTAIN'S SHIELD AND...

CAESAR WOULD SPOT THE FRAUD AT ONCE. AS A MATTER OF COURSE WE'D BE SERVED UP ON THE FAKE SHIELD TO THE LIONS IN THE CIRCUS!

YOU'RE RIGHT... WE'D GET THERE JUST DESSERTS.

I'M SURE THERE MUST BE SOMEONE IN GERGOVIA WHO COULD GIVE US INFORMATION!

THE ARVERNIANS ARE A CAREFUL, CAGEY LOT.

LET'S SEND A SPY! PICK ME A VOLUNTEER!

BONG!

I NOMINATE CAIUS PUSILLANIMUS. THE WORST SKIVER IN THE WHOLE LEGION. I'VE JUST CONFINED HIM TO BARRACKS.

RIGHT. GO AND GET THIS CLASSIC CASE OF YOURS!

PUSILLANIMUS? HE'S ON FATIGUES, SWEEPING THE YARD.

IS THIS YOUR IDEA OF SWEEPING A YARD, PUSILLANIMUS?

HMPH?

LOOK, I'VE SWEPT HALF THE FIRST FLAGSTONE, I'M JUST TAKING A BREATHER, THEN I'LL SWEEP THE OTHER HALF OF THE FIRST FLAGSTONE...

... THEN I'LL TAKE A BREATHER AND GO ON TO THE FIRST HALF OF THE SECOND FLAGSTONE, TAKE A...

TAKE A BREATHER AND COME WITH ME! THE TRIBUNE WANTS TO SEE YOU!

I DON'T LIKE LEAVING A JOB UNFINISHED...

WELL, EVENING ALL! I MUSHT GET ON WITH MY ENQUIRIESH! HIC!

...... MOUSTACHE!

EVENING, ALL! ANY CHANSHE OF A DRINK? HAEC! HOC!

DID YOU HEAR THAT SPY? THE ROMANS ARE LOOKING FOR THE SHIELD OF VERCINGETORIX! THEY MUST NOT FIND IT!

OH, DON'T WORRY... THAT IDIOT WAS ABSOLUTELY STONED...

IT'S UP TO US TO FIND IT! THE TRIUMPH WILL BE OURS, BY TOUTATIS!

PAF!

ASTERIX, THAT'S ALL ANCIENT HISTORY! WE'RE AT PEACE NOW...

BUT I HAVEN'T FINISHED EATING!

COME ALONG, OBELIX. WE'RE OFF TO NEMESSOS STRAIGHT AWAY TO FIND THIS CIRCUMBENDIBUS.

BACK FROM HIS SECRET MISSION, LEGIONARY CAIUS PUSILLANIMUS MAKES HIS REPORT.

AV... AV... EV... EVENING ALL!

?!

WELL? WHAT NEWS?

THEY DON'T KNOW A THING ABOUT ALESHIA... HIC!... BUT THEY KNOW A THING OR TWO ABOUT MAKING WINE, BY SHUPITER!

A REPORT WHICH LANDS HIM STRAIGHT IN CLINK...

NO GOOD BEING KEEN IN THE ARMY. WHAT'S THE USHE OF FLAG-WAGGING? BESHT KEEP YOUR MOUTH SHUT. MATER'SH THE WORD!

EVENING, ALL!

MEANWHILE, OUR FRIENDS HAVE ARRIVED AT THE LARGE ARVERNIAN TOWN OF NEMESSOS*...

※ CLERMONT-FERRAND

BUT HOW DO WE SET ABOUT FINDING CIRCUMBENDIBUS, ASTERIX?

HE MAKES WHEELS... IT SHOULD BE EASY TO SPOT A WHEEL FACTORY...

THERE, LOOK! THE OTHER SIDE OF THAT SQUARE WITH THE STATUE OF JULIUS CAESAR!

COME ALONG!

CIRCVMBENDIBVS WHEELS

CAN I HELP YOU?

WE WANT TO SEE CIRCUMBENDIBUS.

THE BOSS? WHAT ABOUT?

IT'S LIKE THIS... WE'RE LOOKING FOR THE SH...

BONK!

PRIVATE BUSINESS. OUR NAMES ARE ASTERIX AND OBELIX.

AND DOGMATIX.

ASTERIX AND OBELIX WOULD LIKE TO SEE THE BOSS ON PRIVATE BUSINESS.

THAT'S OUR INTERCOM SYSTEM... NOW, IF YOU'D LIKE TO GO INTO THE WAITING ATRIUM...

?

POSH SORT OF PLACE, THIS!

YES, CIRCUMBENDIBUS MUST BE QUITE A WHEELER-DEALER.

LUCIUS CIRCUMBENDIBUS'S PERSONAL ASSISTANT, ANAESTHESIA, WILL SEE YOU NOW. IF YOU'LL JUST COME THIS WAY...

THIS IS OUR CARVING POOL. THE FIRM SELLS WHEELS ALL OVER THE KNOWN WORLD, SO THERE'S A LOT OF STONEWORK...

COME IN!

DO YOU THINK I SHOULD HAVE A CARVING POOL TO SELL MY MENHIRS?

TAP! TAP!

I MIGHT GET TO SELL MY MENHIRS ALL OVER THE KNOWN WORLD, AND...

BELT UP!

THESE ARE THE GENTLEMEN!

THANK YOU, MEMORANDA. YOU MAY GO. NOW, WHAT CAN I DO FOR YOU, GENTLEMEN?

PRIVATE

OBELIX MENHIRS

WE'VE COME TO SEE CIRCUMBENDIBUS.

I'M VERY SORRY, HE'S IN A MEETING AND CANNOT BE DISTURBED. CAN I HELP YOU?

OBELIX DOGMATIX MENHIRS

WE WANT TO SEE CIRCUMBENDIBUS IN PERSON, AT ONCE!

QUITE OUT OF THE QUESTION.

IS THIS HIS DOOR?

YES, THAT'S THE DOOR OF HIS OFFICE, BUT...

PRIVATE

IF YOU'RE AFTER MY GOLD, IT'S IN A CHARCOAL CELLAR IN HELVETIA.

I'M NOT INTERESTED IN YOUR GOLD.

I'VE TOLD YOU WHAT I WANT, BY TOUTATIS! THE CHIEFTAIN'S SHIELD YOU GOT AT ALESIA!

I'M A BIG WHEEL, YOU KNOW; IN MY LINE TIME IS SESTERTII, SO LET'S COME TO THE HUB OF THE MATTER. ARE YOU THREATENING ME?

YES.

I THOUGHT SO. I'LL TELL YOU EVERYTHING. I HAVEN'T GOT THE SHIELD ANY MORE...

YOU'RE RIGHT, I DID GET HOLD OF IT AFTER THE DEFEAT OF VERCINGETORIX.

... BUT IN MY YOUTH I WAS CONSUMED BY THE URGE TO GAMBLE (I JOINED THE LEGION AS THE RESULT OF A SILLY BET)...

HEY, HOW ABOUT A GAME OF RUBER ET NIGER?

... I LOST THE SHIELD TO A LEGIONARY CALLED MARCUS CARNIVERUS IN A GAME OF CHANCE

DIEM PERDIDI!

YOU CAN QUOTE ME ON THAT TOO!

WHEN I WAS DEMOBBED I STAYED IN THESE PARTS AND MADE MY PILE. THE WHEEL OF FORTUNE TURNED MY WAY...

WHERE'S THIS CARNIVERUS NOW?

I THINK HE'S A BATH ATTENDANT AT THE HYDRO IN BORVO ※

?

SHE CALLED THESE PEOPLE, AND THEY WOULDN'T BELIEVE CIRCUMBENDIBUS WAS IN A MEETING, SO I HAD TO DEAL WITH THEM. LOOK, NO HANDS!

WE'RE GOING TO TAKE A COURSE OF TREATMENT!

TREATMENT? WHAT TREATMENT? WHAT FOR?

WE HAVE TO FIND A BATH ATTENDANT AT BORVO, SO DON'T ARGUE. LET'S FIND A FAST CHARIOT TO GET US THERE.

MEANWHILE...

ANAESTHESIA!

YOU GOT THE NAMES OF THOSE BARBARIANS? RIGHT! CARVE A LETTER TO THE OFFICER COMMANDING THE GARRISON OF GERGOVIA AND HAVE IT SENT BY EXPRESS COURIER.

USE A SLAB WITHOUT OUR TABLET-HEAD AND TAKE JUST ONE COPY FOR MY PERSONAL FILES. THIS MESSAGE MUST REMAIN ANONYMOUS AND CONFIDENTIAL.

HERE WE ARE AT BORVO.

BORVO

LISTEN, ASTERIX... DOGMATIX AND I HAVE DECIDED NOT TO HAVE ANY TREATMENT BECAUSE...

OBELIX, THIS IS THE ONLY WAY WE CAN GET INTO THE BATHS AND FIND CARNIVORUS AND THE SHIELD WITHOUT AROUSING SUSPICION!

SO TRY TO LOOK ILL!

IF I DON'T GET A BOAR TO EAT SOON I SHAN'T HAVE TO TRY!

WE'D LIKE TO SEE THE DRUID WHO RUNS THIS HYDRO.

THERAPEUTIX? THIS WAY.

OW THEN, DON'T ORGET TO OOK ILL!

ALL RIGHT, ALL RIGHT, DON'T GO ON ABOUT IT! I GET THE IDEA!

GOOD MORNING, GENTLEMEN.

GOOD MORNING, O DRUID.

OUCH.

DRUID THERAPEUTIX DIRECTOR

WHAT EMS TO BE E TROUBLE?

HE'S ILL. I'M ILL. EVEN OUR DOG IS ILL. WE WANT THE FULL TREATMENT!

LET'S SEE ... DOES IT HURT THERE?

OUCH.

AND THERE?

OUCH.

ELL, THAT'S CLEAR! T'S SAY BATHS AND HOWERS, MASSAGE ND SAUNAS ...

OUCH.

... AND OF COURSE A STRICT DIET.

OUCH!

RIGHT, THE FULL TREATMENT FOR BOTH OF YOU. NOT THE DOG, THOUGH. THE SCIENCE OF HYDROTHERAPY IS STILL IN IT'S INFANCY, AND WE DON'T KNOW IF IT'S GOOD FOR ANIMALS.

ND SO, IN THE COURSE OF TREATMENT, OUR FRIENDS ARE ABLE TO MAKE DISCREET ENQUIRIES ...

HAT'S UR AME?

APPLEJUS

CARROTJUS.

PRUNEJUS.

TOMATOJUS.

THE TREATMENT IS PARTICULARLY PAINFUL AT MEALTIMES ...

YOU'LL BE MARCUS CARNIVERUS, RIGHT?

ER... ER... YES.

WELL, FIRST OF ALL, TWO BOARS IN WINE!

AND TWO FOR ME TOO

V... VER WELL.

HOLD IT RIGHT THERE!

?

I ARREST YOU IN THE NAME OF TRIBUNE NOXIUS VAPUS, SPECIAL ENVOY OF JULIUS CAESAR.

WHAT A PITY... IT WAS SUCH A PRETTY RESTAURANT...

AFTER WE'VE HAD THESE FOR STARTERS, CARNIVERUS, YOU CAN SERVE THE BOARS!

BAOUUH! PAF! POFFF! PIFFF! TCHONC!

WHAT A ROW! THEY SEEM TO BE HAVING QUITE A FLING!

YES... DANCING THE GAULISH FLING TOO, BY THE SOUND OF IT. A FULL HOUSE I'D THINK.

ACK!

YES, THERE YOU ARE.... THEY'RE TURNING PEOPLE AWAY.

NOW, WHERE ARE THOSE BOARS?

THE BOAR IN WINE

AH! AND ABOUT ME TOO! WE'RE THE LAST TO GET WHAT'S COMING TO US!

GOOD! COME AND JOIN US, CARNIVERUS, OLD CHAP.

IT WASN'T MY DOING... AN ANONYMOUS MESSAGE WARNED THEM YOU WERE COMING, AND THEY WERE EXPECTING YOU...

NEVER MIND THAT! JUST HAND OVER THE CHIEFTAIN'S SHIELD AND WE'LL CALL IT QUITS!

THAT'S RIGHT... MUNCH... ANYONE WHO HAS A WAY WITH A BOAR LIKE YOU CAN'T BE ALL BAD!

BUT I HAVEN'T GOT THE SHIELD ANY MORE... I ALREADY TOLD THEM...

...YOU'RE RIGHT, I DID WIN IT IN A GAME OF CHANCE WHEN I WAS A LEGIONARY...

HEY! YOU THERE! QUO VADIS, LADDIE?

...BUT AS I'D LEFT CAMP WITHOUT A PASS I HAD TO GIVE THE SHIELD TO CENTURION TITUS CRAPULUS IN RETURN FOR HIS SILENCE.

O TEMPORA! O MORES!

BLAMBLAMBLAMBLAM.

RIGHT! WHERE'S THIS CRAPULUS THEN?

NOT IN A WATERING PLACE, I HOPE?

THAT GREAT WINESKIN IN A WATERING PLACE? HUH!

NO, HE STAYED IN THE ARMY. THE OTHERS WILL FIND HIM EASILY WHEN THEY CONSULT THE ARMY LISTS; I GAVE THEM HIS NAME.

HOW MUCH DO WE OWE YOU?

12 SESTERTII FOR THE BOARS. THE RESTAURANT'S ON ME. JUST PROMISE YOU'LL NEVER COME BACK.

LATER, AFTER BORROWING A ROMAN CHARIOT WHICH WAS JUST PASSING...

WE MUST GET TO GERGOVIA BEFORE CRAPULUS, TO STOP HIM GIVING THE SHIELD TO THE ROMANS...

IF HE GETS THERE FIRST WE'VE HAD IT. WE CAN'T FIGHT THE WHOLE GARRISON!

WHY NOT? IS OUT OF BOUNDS

LATE THAT NIGHT...

WINES
CHARCOAL

WINESANSPIRIX

WHO... WHO'S THERE?

IT'S US! OBELIX, ASTERIX...

...AND DOGMAT

TOC! TOC!

COME IN, QUICK! THE SKY HAS FALLEN ON OUR HEADS!

?!

AND THERE'S A PRICE ON YOURS, BY THE WAY... THE ROMANS HAVE GONE CRAZY! THEY'RE SEARCHING EVERYWHERE, AND THE WORST OF IT IS...

...MY WINESANSPIRIX HAS DISAPPEARED! NOXIUS VAPUS MUST HAVE TAKEN HIM PRISONER! BOO HOO HOO!

NEVER MIND THE SHIELD! WE'LL FIND YOUR WINESANSPIRIX, BY TOUTATIS!

SNIFF!

YOU CAN BE BOUND WE WILL, EVEN IF THE GARRISON IS OUT OF BOUNDS, BY BELENOS!

AND SO THE OUTLAWED ASTERIX, OBELIX (AND DOGMATIX) SPEND THE NIGHT HIDDEN IN A HEAP OF CHARCOAL...

GOOD NIGHT, OBELIX.

SORRY I LOST MY TEMPER EARLIER YOU'RE A WHITE MAN, ASTERIX!

WAKE UP, ME OLD COCK! YOU'RE GOING TO POT!

HMPH?

THAT'S WHERE YOU'LL END UP TOO, ME BROTH OF A BOY!

COCKADOODLEDO!

COME ON, OBELIX.

LET'S GO AND HAVE A WASH. WE'VE GOT A LOT TO DO TODAY.

OAAAOH.

...TERWARDS...

I'M GOING TO FIND OUT HOW WE CAN GET INTO THE PREFECT'S PALACE UNOBSERVED...

... IF WE MAKE A FORCED ENTRY, WE RISK GETTING WINESANSPIRIX EXECUTED BEFORE WE CAN FREE HIM...

RIGHT. I'M JUST FINISHING MY BATH...

EVERYONE'S BATH!

...ELP! YELP! YELP! YELP! PFFF! PFFF!

IT'S ALL FIXED, OBELIX! I'VE FOUND A WAY OF GETTING INTO THE PALACE.

WINESANSPIRIX

WINES CHARCOAL

THIS IS THERMOSTATIX, WINESANSPIRIX'S BROTHER-IN-LAW. HE'S DELIVERING SOME CHARCOAL TO THE PALACE...

WE CAN HIDE IN THE CHARCOAL.

WELL, I WASN'T TO KNOW, WAS I?

GRRRRR GRR

41

43

YOU CAN COME OUT NOW. THE ROMANS THINK YOU'VE LEFT GERGOVIA. THEY'RE SEARCHING THE FOREST.

LATER, AFTER A QUICK WASH AND *BRUSH UP*...

NOW THEN, WHAT'S ALL THIS ABOUT, WINESANSPIRIX?

WELL, IT'S LIKE THIS... I WAS SELLING WINE IN ALESIA...

... AND THE NIGHT AFTER ALESIA WAS TAKEN A CENTURION CAME TO MY PLACE... A REAL OLD SOAK...

WINESANSPIRIX WINES CHARCOAL

... I SWOPPED HIM AN AMPHORA OF WINE FOR THE CHIEFTAIN'S SHIELD...

AND THEN A GAULISH WARRIOR WHO WAS ABOUT TO LEAVE FOR HOME SAW THE SHIELD

LET'S HAVE A LOOK AT THAT SHIELD!

... AND HE BEGGED ME TO LET HIM HAVE IT FOR SAFE KEEPING.

WELL, IF IT GIVES YOU ANY SATISFACTION...

SO IN A WEAK MOMENT I GAVE THAT GLORIOUS SHIELD TO A STRANGER WHO DIDN'T EVEN COME FROM THESE PARTS!

CHEER UP, WINESANSPIRIX. FAR BE IT FROM US TO CAST THE FIRST MENHIR ※...

※ PEOPLE WITHOUT POT CAST SMALLER STONES

AND WHEN I SAW HOW IMPORTANT THE SHIELD IS TO YOU I WAS ASHAMED OF MYSELF, AND I RAN AWAY. THEN I WAS OVERCOME WITH REMORSE AND CAME BACK TO CONFESS...

CAN YOU REMEMBER THE WARRIOR'S NAME?

NO, HE WAS RATHER THIN AND RATHER UNHAPPY, THAT'S ALL I...

THAT'S HIM!!!

?

O ROMANS!

WHAT'S UP?

OH, NOTHING... DON'T TAKE ANY NOTICE...

THE TRIUMPH OF CHIEF VITALSTATISTIX ON THE SHIELD OF VERCINGETORIX!

AKE A GOOD OOK! AND YOU, RAVE PEOPLE OF ERGOVIA, COME AND ATCH OUR TRIUMPH!

RIGHT. VENI, VIDI, AND I GET THE IDEA. NO ONE MUST EVER KNOW I SAW THIS... AND AS I CANNOT CONGRATULATE YOU ON THE CURIOUS APPEARANCE OF YOUR TROOPS...

... AND SO AS TO MAKE SURE MY VISIT REMAINS A SECRET, I'M SENDING YOU AND YOUR MEN TO A GARRISON IN NUMIDIA...

AH! AT LAST! TWO CLEAN SOLDIERS!

HIC!

HIC!

CENTURION! I PROMOTE YOU TO OFFICER COMMANDING THE GARRISON OF GERGOVIA! LEGIONARY, I PROMOTE YOU TO CENTURION! AND I NEVER WANT TO HEAR THE NAME OF THIS TOWN AGAIN! AVE!

AVE! DON'T YOU WORRY, WE'LL KEEP ON THE BEST OF TERMS WITH THE WINE MERCHANTS OF THESE PARTS, ME AND PUSILLANIMUS.

CENTURION PUSILLAN — HIC! — MUS!

OUR FRIENDS ARE QUITE SORRY TO LEAVE GERGOVIA AFTER THEIR MEMORABLE TRIUMPH...

ON THE WAY HOME THE CHIEF'S STATISTICS REVITALIZED AS HE VISITS ALL THE INNS PATRONIZED ON THE OUTWARD JOURNEY

OUR VILLAGE!

AND ONCE AGAIN OUR STORY ENDS WITH A BANQUET... EVERYONE IS THERE. EVERYONE? NO, SOMEONE IS MISSING... WHO CAN IT BE?

NOT HIM; HE'S THERE ALL RIGHT. SO WHO CAN IT BE, THEN?

...WHO?

BUT, IMPEDIMENTA, I HAVE TO SIT AT THE HEAD OF THE TABLE! I HAVE TO GO! I'M CURED, MY LOVE

IMPEDIMENTA! YOU'RE NOT GOING TO HIT ME OVER THE HEAD WITH THAT SHIELD, ARE YOU?!?

THE END

UDERZO & GOSCINNY

PRINTED IN BELGIUM BY proost INTERNATIONAL BOOK PRODUCTION